Elephant's music

Monika Filipina

P9-DGZ-888

Books for Kids From the
American Psychological Association
maginationpress.org

Original title: La musica di Ettore © Camelozampa, Italy, 2020
Copyright © 2021 by Magination Press, an imprint of the American Psychological Association.
All rights reserved. Except as permitted under the United States Copyright Act of 1976, no part of this publication may be reproduced or distributed in any form or by any means, or stored in a database or retrieval system, without the prior written permission of the publisher.

Magination Press is a registered trademark of the American Psychological Association.
Order books at maginationpress.org, or call 1-800-374-2721.

Book design by Rachel Ross
Printed by Sonic Media Solutions, Inc., Medford, NY

Library of Congress Cataloging-in-Publication Data
Names: Filipina, Monika, author.
Title: Elephant's music/Monika Filipina.
Other titles: Musica di Ettore. English
Description: [Washington, D.C.]: Magination Press, [2021] | Summary:
   Unable to play an instrument, Edward the elephant resigns himself to
   being a good audience for the jungle band, but when he is running late
   for a concert one day, his musical talent is revealed.
Identifiers: LCCN 2020032645 (print) | LCCN 2020032646 (ebook) | ISBN
   9781433835056 (hardback) | ISBN 9781433835704 (ebook)
Subjects: CYAC: Musicians—Fiction. | Bands (Music)—Fiction. |
                Ability—Fiction. | Elephants—Fiction. | Jungle animals—Fiction.
                Classification: LCC PZ7.1.F5334 Ele 2021 (print) | LCC PZ7.1.F5334
                   (ebook) | DDC [E]—dc23
                LC record available at https://lccn.loc.gov/2020032645
                LC ebook record available at https://lccn.loc.gov/2020032646

            Manufactured in the United States of America
         10 9 8 7 6 5 4 3 2 1

Elephant's music

Monika Filipina

Magination Press • Washington, DC • American Psychological Association

Once upon a time there was a jungle,

and in the jungle there lived animals.

Everyone could play an instrument

and make beautiful music.

Everyone except Edward.

The only thing that Edward could
make was a terrible noise.

And although he tried...

...he always ruined the song.

So instead Edward became the band's biggest fan and never missed any concerts.

But one day he woke up very late for their concert.

Edward ran as fast
as he could.

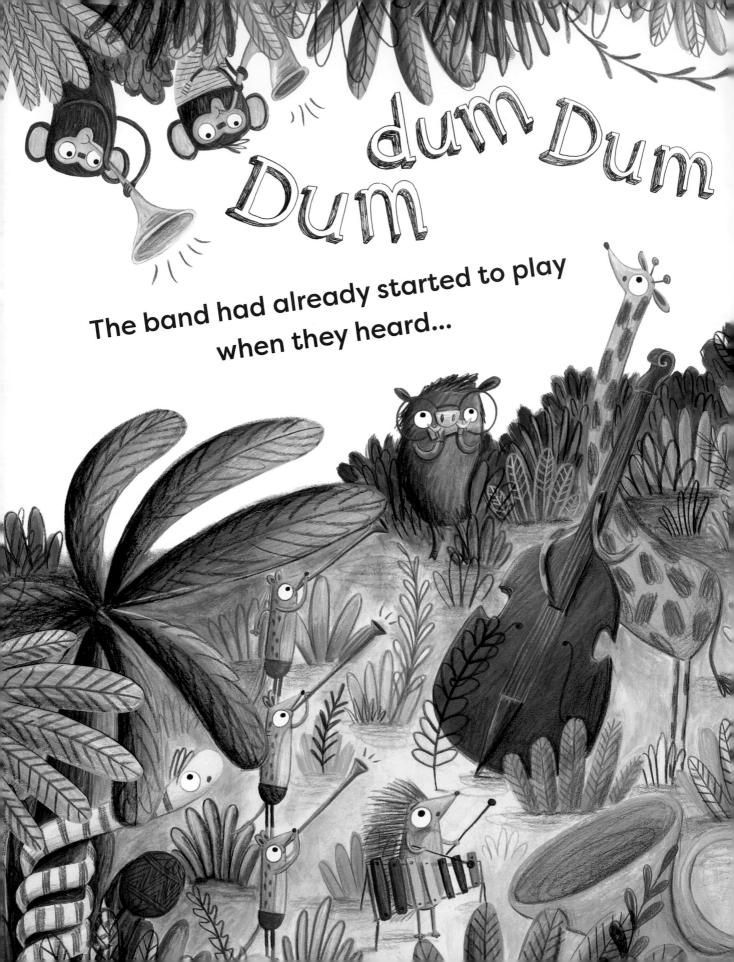

dum Dum

Dum

Dum

The band had already started to play when they heard...

Dum D

It got louder and louder...

um DUM

and their music sounded better and better! What was this sound?

... It was Edward!

The monkeys
had an
amazing idea.

Now Edward
is in the
band too!

MONIKA FILIPINA is an award winning author and illustrator. She completed her Master's Degree in Children's Book Illustration at Cambridge School of Arts. She lives in Toruń, Poland.

f @MonikaFilipinaIllustration

🐦 📷 @MonikaFilipina

MAGINATION PRESS is the children's book imprint of the American Psychological Association. APA works to advance psychology as a science and profession and as a means of promoting health and human welfare. Magination Press books reach young readers and their parents and caregivers to make navigating life's challenges a little easier. It's the combined power of psychology and literature that makes a Magination Press book special.

Visit maginationpress.org

f 🐦 📷 📌 @MaginationPress